SECRET OF ZARB

Titles in this series

BASIL DEAKIN

SECRET OF ZARB

Collins
LONDON AND GLASGOW

First published 1967

© *Wm. Collins Sons & Co., Ltd. 1967*

PRINTED AND MADE IN GREAT BRITAIN BY
WM. COLLINS SONS AND CO. LTD.
LONDON AND GLASGOW

Chapter One

"STAND BY to jump!"

The warning words crackled over the plane's intercom. In the dim light of the cabin behind the control cockpit two figures tensed. They were Greg Grayson, crack undercover agent to WASP, the World Association for Security and Peace, and his assistant Steve Stanton.

"We're all set," Greg quietly remarked and Steve nodded while his fingers ran deftly over the parachute strapped to his body.

"Black as pitch out there," the pilot's voice came through to them, a note of satisfaction in its tone. "Not much risk you'll be spotted as you flutter to earth. Good luck."

"Thanks," Greg called back. "All set to go."

His eyes were fixed on the warning light. It was red. When the pilot was exactly over the dropping zone, the light would change to green.

Below in the dark lay Batania, deep in

the central Continent. Surrounded by friendly countries, Batania had gradually cut itself off from its neighbours by erecting frontier posts, barriers of tangled wire and mined stretches of no-man's land.

WASP was worried by these mysterious events. It had alerted Greg and his co-operator, Steve, to make a secret parachute jump by night into Batania, to contact a British secret service agent living there in the guise of a mountain guide.

"Bell, our chap in Batania, should know something of what's going on behind its closed frontiers," Greg had been told. "We've arranged to drop you two under-cover agents in the mountains near his cabin."

"Green light on!"

One of the aircrew swung back a trap in the cabin floor. The wind screamed loudly in Greg's ears as, with one final glance at Steve to make sure he was ready to follow at once, he started to drop through the trap.

His hand suddenly flashing towards Steve, Greg thrust a small pin into Steve's windcheater; then with a brief wave to the aircrew, he vanished into the night.

Steve dropped after him and within seconds the high-flying plane was roaring into the distance, its engines fading to silence. Greg shot one glance upward as his parachute opened out above him. Vaguely he saw Steve's 'chute spreading wide, then his gaze swept downward. His brow creased in puzzlement.

The clouds below him had a strange orange glow, as though a forest fire was casting its glare on their under layers. His pulses quickened. Could that be it? Were they dropping through the thick belt of clouds into an inferno of blazing mountain trees?

The clamminess of the clouds closed round him and Steve vanished from his view, as in almost complete silence Greg sank rapidly earthward. As he fell, the orange glow became rapidly brighter.

Suddenly Greg was through the clouds and his eyes widened in startled dismay.

It was not the glow of a fire which was lighting the underside of the clouds. The bright lights of hundreds of street lamps lay below. He and Steve were floating down to the rooftops of a large city.

" The pilot must have been off course,"

Greg gasped under his breath. "Instead of dropping us in the mountains near Bell's cabin, he's flown us over Lonz, the biggest city in Batania."

His gaze raked the streets below. They appeared deserted. It was long past midnight. Most of the Lonz citizens would be in bed and asleep. Greg breathed more easily. With luck, he and Steve might make a safe and unseen landing in Lonz.

A large garden loomed beneath him. He jerked on his lines and the 'chute swung him steadily towards the garden and its wide stretch of open lawn. Greg darted an anxious skyward glance for sight of Steve.

There was no sign of him! Before Greg could jerk his head round to look over his shoulder, the ground was rushing up at him. He bunched his legs and with a rush he was down, rolling over, pulling in his lines.

Coolly but rapidly he unbuckled his harness. Rolling the 'chute into a tight bundle, he sped lightly to a compost heap, broke it open with his hands and quickly buried the bundled 'chute.

"Where's Steve?" he murmured to him-

Suddenly Greg was through the clouds . . .

self, anxiously looking round. "Must have made a landing by now, because he was out of the kite right behind me."

He flicked a pin-head projection in his wrist-watch. From the watch came a barely audible buzz. Greg's eyes gleamed with relief. The faint buzz being transmitted through his wrist-watch came from the locator pin Greg had fastened to Steve's windcheater before they jumped.

Stealthily he crept from the garden into the lamp-lit street. The buzz although low in volume, was becoming steadily louder as Greg used it to steer his steps. It was leading him in the direction of the locator pin.

He came to a square overlooked by a large church. The square was empty and bathed in light from the lamps surrounding it. Greg's micro-transmitter was now buzzing with increased urgency. Steve must be near.

A floodlight in front of the church shone upwards and the steeple stood out brilliantly against the night sky. Greg's eyes popped in startled dismay.

Steve was suspended on the steeple by his parachute which was hooked over its towering spire. He hung there, a helpless prisoner, waving frantically to attract Greg's attention.

Greg gave a start. He had heard the low hum of a slow-moving vehicle approaching the square. It was almost certain to be a police patrol car and its occupants were sure to see Steve draped on the steeple.

He acted without a moment's hesitation. He sped to the front of the floodlight and raising his foot smashed its glass front and kicked in its powerful electric globe, plunging the steeple into shadow. Steve was now only a dark smudge high on the steeple.

The approaching car revved up and Greg knew that the crash of breaking glass had been heard by its occupants. He must get them away from the square before they started to investigate.

Making as much noise as he could with his shoes, Greg broke into a run. Over his shoulder he saw the patrol car spurt into the square and come after him.

Darting round a corner, Greg tore off his shoes and raced on in his stockinged feet. Bursting round another corner he saw that the street was lined with lime trees.

At monkey speed he shinned up the first he

came to and crouched in the depths of its leafy branches. He watched with a brief grin as the patrol car sped by below.

Dropping to the ground, still in his socks, he noiselessly raced back to the square, halting at the foot of the steeple. Steve was still there, helpless and still.

In a few moments Greg, using the lock-pick tool which had so often opened almost impossible locks, was pushing wide the small door at the foot of the steeple. Hastily donning his shoes, he climbed the circular stairway at top speed until he reached a small platform. He could go no higher.

A narrow window was before him, blotted out by the taut folds of Steve's parachute. Using his sheath knife Greg carefully cut a hole through the 'chute, pushed his head out and peered up and down.

Steve was hanging below. It was impossible to pull him to safety through one of the slit windows; they were too narrow. He would have to get him down, stage by stage —if the patrol car did not return to prevent him!

Racing back down the steps, Greg halted at the window below. He reached out, slashed through one of the nylon lines of Steve's harness and tied it firmly to the stone centre-post of the narrow window, leaving Steve suspended level with a window below.

Then he cut all the other lines until Steve hung by the one line he had tied to the window post, while the freed lines fell down the steeple.

Speeding down to the lower window, Greg tied one of the loose lines to that window bar, then slashed through the line by which Steve hung from the upper window. Gripping the line he had just tied, he lowered Steve to its full length down the side of the steeple.

Once again he hurtled down the steps to the next window. Again he tied a line of the 'chute to a window support, cut through the line holding Steve to the upper window and lowered him to the next one below.

Stage by stage Greg lowered his friend until he heard a gasp of relief, and Steve called to him in a whisper that he was only a few feet from the ground.

Greg slashed the last of the nylon lines, and as Steve dropped on his toes at the foot of the towering steeple, Greg raced out of its low door.

"Thanks, pal," Steve grinned. Mopping his face, he looked up at the shadowy shrouds of the 'chute hanging from the crest of the steeple. "I felt a right Charlie hanging up there."

"Listen," Steve rapped, cocking an ear. "That patrol's returning. Quick, into those bushes beside the church's outer wall."

They dived into the depths of the bushes just as the patrol car appeared in the square and drove up to the front of the church.

"What's happened to the floodlight?" the hidden undercover agents heard one of the car's crew ask loudly.

The uniformed figure climbed from the car and walked to the floodlight. He yelled to the others in the car that it was smashed, that it was the floodlight they had heard breaking.

One of the crew swivelled the car's powerful searchlight towards the church and then to the steeple. As the light climbed Greg and Steve heard a startled shout. The 'chute was revealed dangling from the spire.

"Parachutist!" They heard the bellow.

"A spy has landed—and escaped. There may be others. Radio all patrols to set up road blocks to stop them getting out of Lonz. Stop all cars and pedestrians."

Steve clenched his fists. They *had* to get out of Lonz without delay, to make their way to the mountain cabin where Bell, WASP's secret agent in Batania, was living in the guise of a mountain guide. They must reach him without delay to try to discover what was happening in Batania, behind its closed and fortified frontier.

The patrol car's crew had climbed out to gape up at the wrecked parachute high on the spire. They were standing with their backs to the car parked in the roadway outside the church.

"After me," Greg whispered, carefully parting the bushes. Doubled low, he ran to the car.

He slipped into the driver's seat and seconds later Steve was beside him. Letting in the clutch, Greg put his foot hard down on the accelerator and the car burst away from the kerbside. Startled yells from the car crew rang in their ears as the men started to run after the car.

" Ahead !" Steve shouted. " Road block !"

A car was drawn across the road, all but blocking it. Greg's jaw tightened. He thumbed down a switch and from the front bumper a raucous siren shrieked into the silence of the night.

" Wow—they're getting out of the way," Steve gasped, a chuckle in his voice. " Keep it up, Greg. This is one car they won't halt, 'cos it's one of their own."

With the streets empty of traffic, Greg roared out of Lonz. But how long would it be before other patrol cars were warned by radio that this car contained two spies?

" Daylight," Steve muttered. As the car tore into the mountains, the first streaks of dawn were lighting the sky. " How much farther . . . ?"

He lurched forward as Greg slammed down the brakes. In their path, at a hair-pin bend, a car blocked the road, a machine-gun poised above its bonnet.

"Out," Greg roared as a burst of gun-fire smashed the silence and bullets whined round them.

Leaping clear of the car on to the side of the mountain road, the two agents burst

A burst of gunfire smashed the silence . . .

through bushes and raced up the slope. Pounding footsteps on the hard surface of the road warned them that the car's crew was after them.

A metallic clanking caught Greg's ear. It came from somewhere above them, far up the thickly wooded slope. At a fast climb he led Steve in its direction.

Swinging above the trees, they caught sight of an overhead ropeway. At intervals girders, blocks of stone, wooden posts, coils of barbed wire swung along above them and disappeared over folds in the mountain.

Steve made a hasty calculation with a tiny compass.

"That ropeway runs in the direction of Bell's mountain cabin," he told Greg rapidly. And next instant he was pushing through the thick trees and scrub towards a tall steel pylon.

The pylon was one of an endless chain of similar pylons carrying the ropeway. Greg began to climb it and Steve hastened after him.

Clinging to it, just below the endless ropeway, Greg watched the next load come swinging along in their direction. It was a massive length of timber, thick as a man's body.

"When it reaches us," he said to Steve, "get astride it on one side of the clamp holding it to the ropeway. I'll slither on to the other end, to balance it. Ready—mount up, cowboy," he added with a chuckle.

Acting together, they swung away from the pylon, gripped either side of the clamp and throwing their legs over the balk of timber, landed astride it facing each other.

The ropeway spun steadily over treetops, across a shallow valley, dipped through towering pines and on over the rising slopes of the mountainside.

Gradually the trees thinned and into view came a narrow roadway. Greg snapped a sudden warning to Steve.

"Motor-cycle and sidecar on the road . . . and the sidecar's got a machine gun mounted. Must be a patrol."

Tensely they eyed the armed sidecar and the two men aboard the vehicle while the ropeway swept them steadily closer to the road.

The rider in the sidecar suddenly lifted his head. He was eyeing the ropeway and

Greg saw him pointing. He had spotted the two figures squatting astride the length of timber. A pair of binoculars were being trained upon them and next moment the pair saw the man drop the binoculars and swing up his machine-gun.

"Swing off the log," Greg roared, "and hang on the ropeway."

The gun rat-a-tat-tatted but the gunner's aim was spoiled by the bouncing of the motor-cycle's wheels on the rough surface of the narrow mountain road. Bullets screamed past Greg and Steve and smashed into the log as the two hurled themselves from the timber on to the ropeway.

The length of timber was now directly above the road up which the motor-cycle and sidecar spurted. The gunner, swaying in his seat, continued to fire wildly.

Greg's hand flashed to the clamp gripping the lock and snapped open its jaws. The heavy length of timber dropped, hitting the road below with a thud. It bounced once, crashed into the sidecar and overturned it. Both men were hurled on to the road, where they lay stunned.

"Down," Greg gasped, swinging off the

ropeway on to a pylon at the edge of the road. At breakneck speed he hurled himself down its steel girdering, reached the ground and raced across to the overturned combination.

With a powerful heave he righted it. Its engine was still running. Steve had now landed on the road and without a word vaulted into the sidecar. Greg opened the throttle and the motor-cycle leapt up the road.

"This is the mountain track leading to Bell's cabin," Greg shouted above the noise of the engine, and Steve answered with a nod. "Hope he's still there. WASP's secret radio message in code to Bell alerted him that we'd be at his cabin last night."

Steve watched the track ahead anxiously, ready to use the sidecar's machine-gun if necessary. By now, they both knew, every patrol in the mountains of Batania must have been informed that two daring and desperate foreign agents had penetrated into Batania.

Greg slowed and swung the machine off the roadway at the foot of a steep, rocky track. Hurriedly they both dismounted and pushed the motor-cycle into thick bush, hiding it completely from the roadway.

"Up this track," Greg said and at a fast climbing rate he pushed forward, Steve hard on his heels, until, on a small plateau, they saw the cabin.

Cautiously, from a clump of trees, they examined it. A figure stepped out on the cabin's porch, shading his eyes as he surveyed the mountainside and the track.

"Okay," Greg said with satisfaction. "That's Bell. Seems he's looking to see if we're coming."

As Greg and Steve appeared from the trees Bell, dressed as a mountain guide, ran to greet them.

"What detained you two?" he grinned at them. "Thought you were dropping in last night," and they chuckled at his humorous reference to their parachute jumps.

Briefly Greg related what had happened. Bell's expression changed as he listened.

"Then ZARB is on to you," he rapped, and they stared at him questioningly, wondering what he meant by ZARB. He hastened to explain. "ZARB is the Batanian word for leader; and ZARB is the most ruthless and evil leader the deluded people of Batania have ever had. He has them completely in his power—helped by his murderous army of thugs who call themselves soldiers."

"Bad as that?" Greg muttered grimly. "But why has he barricaded the frontiers and kicked out all foreigners? What is he up to, Bell? That's what we've come here to find out."

Bell, one-time war pilot, now secret agent for WASP in Batania, stared back at Greg with a grim look.

"ZARB has the most fearful ambition," he snapped. "He is scheming to become not only the leader of Batania, but of the whole of the central Continent. And for that purpose he has secret agents scattered all over the world."

He paused, head tilted, as though listening.

"Thought I heard something out there, on the mountain," he rapped and stepped to the door to gaze over the plateau and its ring of trees. "H'm, must have imagined it. Listen, Greg. This is what I do know."

He took a deep breath.

"ZARB has secretly summoned his agents

back to Batania. They will be arriving at the Lonz airport some time to-day. To-morrow he has a secret meeting arranged, when he will brief his agents and give them their orders."

Greg stared at him with rising excitement.

In an urgent voice he snapped, " What orders? And where is the secret meeting to be held? Do you know the answers, Bell?"

" Yes!" Bell nodded his head. " Yes, I know, Greg. The meeting is to take place at . . ."

He broke off, spinning on his heels to stare out of the window behind him as a sudden, tearing whoosh thundered over the plateau, drowning his last words.

Greg, facing the window, let out a yell of warning as he hurled himself at Bell, throwing him to the floor while Steve dived after them.

The mortar bomb which Greg had sighted whizzing out of the trees, sped down towards the cabin on the plateau and exploded with a shattering crunch on the heavily timbered roof above them.

The beams crashed down on the three figures spread-eagled on the cabin floor, splintered glass showering wickedly round them, timbers bursting over their heads.

Greg dazedly thrust a splintered beam aside, staggered to his feet and stooped over Bell. Steve was struggling up, shaking his head to clear it. He heard Greg utter a groan of dismay.

"Bell's unconscious," Greg grated. "Beam of timber cracked down on his head. He may be out for hours, could be days . . . and the secret meeting he spoke of is to-morrow."

He spun round and clambered over the debris to the wrecked doorway. Steve heard his hiss of alarm.

"We're surrounded," he rasped through dust-caked lips. "ZARB's patrols are closing in on the plateau to complete the destruction their mortar bomb started. They're coming in for the kill, Steve."

Chapter Two

THE SHATTERED DOORWAY concealed Greg from the Batanian killers surging out of the trees below the plateau. He darted to the rear of the mortar-torn cabin, and after a hasty glance at the steep forest-covered slope rising behind it, Greg flipped open a nylon case strapped to his shin.

Swiftly he fitted together a long, thin alloy tube and a tiny cylinder of compressed air. He then slipped a slim dart into the upper end of the cylinder.

Taking careful aim, Greg released the compressed air. Its pressure sent the dart zooming far into the trees.

"Greg," Steve called to him through a shattered window at the back of the cabin, "those armed thugs in soldiers' uniforms are going to rush the plateau. What about Bell? He's out cold."

Greg nodded as he put a fountain pen to his lips. Steve saw him speaking into its head, and knew that it was a micro-transmitter with a powerful range of amplification.

From the dart, buried in the bark of one of the distant trees, echoed a distant shout, tinged with fear.

"Hurry, we've got to make our escape while they are searching the wrecked cabin. Run, chaps, run for your lives."

It was Greg's voice transmitting a phoney escape alert and Steve tensed, waiting to see if Greg's desperate ruse would succeed. Would the men now running towards the foot of the plateau race past the cabin, believing their quarry had escaped from it and were already deep in the forest behind?

"By thunder, they've bought it," he hissed excitedly. "They believe we got away before that mortar bomb hit the cabin. They're chasing past the cabin, making for the trees on the slope behind."

Bell lay still on the floor. Greg made a rapid examination and his expression was grave. The beam which had crashed down on Bell had knocked him into deep unconsciousness. He might be out for days!

"The bike is at the bottom of the track," he stated rapidly. "We've got to get Bell to hospital. Can't leave him here. He needs a doctor's attention."

Steve looked at Greg grimly. Bell had been on the point of telling them where the meeting of ZARB's agents would take place and what ZARB's orders would be—but the mortar bomb had smashed down a second before he could give them this vital information.

Now, however perilous their own situation, they could not leave Bell in the ruined cabin to fall into the hands of ZARB's ruthless agents.

Greg was already on his knees, lifting Bell on to his broad shoulders. Stooping under the weight, he climbed over the timbers of the wrecked cabin to its shattered door.

" Okay, Steve," he breathed. " Let's make a run for it before they discover they've been fooled."

Bending low, Bell's heavy frame on his back, and with Steve in the rear keeping a look-out for ZARB's killers, Greg went as fast as he could across the plateau and dropped down on to the track.

Slithering, stumbling and almost tripping over small boulders, Greg at last staggered to a halt and lowered Bell to the ground.

Pulling the bushes apart, he wheeled the motor-cycle and sidecar from its hiding-place.

"Into the sidecar," he rapped, then lowered Bell on to Steve's lap. "We whipped past a hospital on the outskirts of Lonz. I spotted its lighted sign when we skimmed out of the city last night."

They both knew the risk they were running in returning to Lonz, but neither gave it more than a fleeting thought. Bell had urgent need of a doctor; after which they must at all costs discover where ZARB was to hold his secret meeting.

Greg set off along the narrow mountain road. Steve sat grimly fingering the machine-gun mounted on the front of the sidecar, ready to use it without hesitation. But no attempts were made to halt the combination as it roared into the outskirts of Lonz and its now busy streets.

Greg swept through the gates of the hospital, climbed a short slope beneath a raised terrace and brought the machine to a halt in front of the hospital.

"Our friend's had an accident," Greg said in perfect Batanian to the first person they met. "We'd like a doctor to examine him at once, please."

The orderly whom he had addressed instantly led them to a small room. Greg and Steve, carrying the unconscious man, followed. The orderly left them and a few minutes later a doctor entered. He bent over to examine Bell.

"Nothing serious," he stated at last, to their immense relief, then added, "but he'll have to stay here for a couple of days until he's fully recovered."

Greg gave a start of dismay. "How long is he likely to be unconscious?" he asked.

"Could be to-morrow or the next day, can't be certain. Don't worry, he'll be all right in our hands." And with that the doctor ushered them from the room.

Greg halted in the entrance hall and spoke hurriedly in an undertone to Steve.

"We've got to find out where ZARB is holding his meeting without waiting for Bell to recover consciousness. All we know is that the meeting is for to-morrow."

Steve saw him give a sudden start, a gleam of hope in his face.

"Bell said the agents were flying in from

all parts of the world and landing at Lonz airport. That's where we'll make a start, Steve. If we can pick out one of ZARB's agents we can trail him to the meeting-place."

He turned to hurry from the hospital, brushing past a man in the doorway who had been there when they had carried Bell in. To Steve's surprise Greg walked past the motor-cycle, but a steely glance from his companion warned him that there must be a good reason. They strode down the slope below the terrace and out of the hospital gates into the street.

"We're running a terrible risk," Steve breathed. "ZARB's police and his plain-clothes agents will be on the alert for the two spies who dropped by parachute into Lonz. And now we haven't even the bike and sidecar. . . ." His voice trailed off.

Greg was not listening. He was fingering a gold signet ring on his left hand. Steve saw him press its square face, revealing a tiny concave mirror which had been hidden under the gold-faced front.

Raising his left arm, as though to look at his wrist watch, Greg darted a quick glance at the mirror. It showed him the pavement behind them.

"Good, just as I thought," he murmured. "We're being trailed by that chap who was in the hospital entrance. Steve, get ready to work our tracker trick when we get round the next corner."

Steve flashed him a brief grin and nodded.

The instant they were round the corner Greg darted into a doorway while Steve sped on and fell into step alongside a man who, from the rear, bore some resemblance in height and dress to the back view of Greg.

Greg, falling into the trail well behind their unsuspecting tracker, saw Steve turning towards the stranger as though he was in conversation with him. Greg smiled to himself.

The trail continued until a phone box was reached. Steve passed it, still appearing to talk to the man at his side. Their tracker strode after them. As Greg reached the phone box he slipped into it.

Swiftly he pressed a metal disc the size of a button under the coin box and again stepped out into the street.

Greg watched Steve turn away from his

companion and swing round. His tracker halted and Greg saw his startled expression. It rapidly changed to one of anger and dismay as he realised that he had been tricked.

Greg leapt into a doorway as the tracker spun on his heels and dashed to the telephone kiosk. Sliding into a nearby passageway between two shops, Greg put his watch to his ear, turned a micro-sized control knob and switched on the miniature transistor receiver hidden under its works.

"Kay five here," Greg heard, as the tracker spoke into the phone. His voice was being picked up by Greg's microphone-transmitter hidden under the coin box. "An injured man has just been taken into hospital by two men on a motor-cycle. I was trailing them. One's got away. The other one's outside looking for him. Suspect the two spies."

"Right," Greg heard the snapped reply. "We'll get the injured man from the hospital. An ambulance will go to collect him immediately. Meanwhile, you . . ."

But Greg did not wait to hear more. Bell was to be seized by ZARB's agents. Somehow he must prevent that happening. It would mean Bell's death if he was captured.

He made an urgent sign to Steve who raced to his side.

"Back to the hospital," he gritted. "Got to get Bell out of there at once. ZARB's agents know he's there."

Hurrying through the now crowded streets they made all the haste they could back to the hospital. Striding up the slope alongside the terrace which overlooked it, they came in sight of the hospital doorway. An ambulance stood there, its rear doors open.

"ZARB hasn't wasted any time," Steve gasped.

"If it's here to collect Bell, then you're right," came Greg's grim answer. "Come on, Steve."

They slipped into the entrance hall. Greg hurried to the reception desk to ask where Bell was.

"Top floor, private ward," was the reply, "but he's being transferred to another hospital. The ambulance men have gone up to collect him."

The two undercover agents strode quickly to the lifts. One of the two lifts was at the top. They darted into the other and shot to the top floor. Half-a-dozen doors to private wards faced them.

"He must be in one of them," Greg rapped. "Look into each until we find him. We'll have to clobber the phoney ambulance men and get Bell out quickly, whether he's conscious or not. We've got to save him from ZARB."

Moments later Greg and Steve faced one another. Every room was empty. Bell was gone. Greg spun round and eyed the lifts. Both had returned to the ground floor.

"One of 'em must have been going down while we were coming up," he said in a cold rage. "And it must have had Bell in it."

"And the other lift reset itself and returned to ground level while we searched the rooms," Steve rapped, while he looked for a stairway.

Greg raced to the window and looked out.

"Steve," he yelled over his shoulder, "they are putting Bell on a stretcher into the ambulance. Before we can find the stairs they'll be off and away."

He was running his eyes round the top landing, desperately seeking a way to halt the ambulance before it started down the slope leading out of the grounds. Steve heard him utter a sharp gasp, then Greg was running along the corridor, halting in front of a steel trap in the wall. Above it was a sign in Batanian.

Below the trap was what looked like a telescopic fire hose, but it was much larger in circumference.

"Got it," Greg said triumphantly. "It's a fire-escape chute," and even as he spoke he was opening the trap and pulling the release handle. Instantly the chute streaked down at a steep slant, held rigid by telescopic metal ridges.

"Into the chute, Steve," Greg snapped, and as Steve slid feet first and shot out of sight down the interior of the chute, Greg was already following him.

They swept down the dark interior and landed with a thud at the foot of the chute, Greg crashing into Steve as he was so close behind him.

Jerking to their feet, they sprinted to the front of the building. Steve groaned in dismay and slackened pace. The ambulance was no longer there. But Greg raced on, making for the terrace which overlooked the slope leading to the gate.

The ambulance was rolling down the slope. Greg hurtled across the terrace, Steve pounding after him, wondering what Greg was planning to do.

He saw Greg gather himself, leap and land on the roof of the ambulance. He fell his full length along it. Without hesitation, Steve too jumped from the terrace, landing spread-eagled alongside Greg.

The noise of their landing had been effectively drowned by the clamour of the ambulance's siren as it demanded free passage at the hospital gate. The roof must also have been reinforced, Greg thought fleetingly, for the occupants not to have felt the shock of two falling bodies.

"Hang on to the sign on the roof," Greg gasped, as the swing and surge of the vehicle seemed likely to hurl them from the smooth-topped roof. Grimly both men gripped the ambulance sign above the windscreen.

Gasps of astonishment and startled yells at the ambulance driver from people on the pavements were ignored—the ambulance was past before their signals and shouts could be seen or heard.

Out of Lonz it raced and up a steep hill at the top of which was a sharp bend. Here it slowed down.

"By heck, look," Greg hissed.

The ambulance was approaching the drawbridge to a massive castle. Armed sentries guarded the narrow gateway under a raised portcullis on the far side of the drawbridge. The ambulance was slowing to cross the bridge.

Greg let go his hold on the sign and hastily slid backwards, nudging Steve to do the same. Together they slipped off the back and dropped to the ground. The ambulance hid them from the sentries as they fled back to the sharp bend in the road.

"Steve," Greg gasped, "that castle must be ZARB's headquarters; that's why there are armed sentries. This must be the place where ZARB will meet his agents who are flying in from all over the world tomorrow."

Steve didn't answer. He knew Greg must be right; but how could they get into the castle? Its grim battlemented walls were surrounded by a deep moat, and its only entrance across the drawbridge was heavily guarded. His thoughts flashed to Bell.

Greg knew what he was thinking. Not only had they to discover the reason for the next day's secret meeting, they had now also to rescue Bell and save him from certain death at the hands of ZARB, the ruthless leader and ruler of Batania.

"It's still the airport for us," he breathed, a glint in his eyes which raised Steve's hopes as he saw it. "ZARB's agents will be landing there to-day. We've got to get to the airport before they leave for ZARB's castle HQ."

They broke into a run, flashing down the steep road until they came to the highway leading into Lonz. Slowing to a fast walk, they strode through the outskirts of the city until, with a mutter of relief, Greg spied an empty taxicab. He signalled it to the kerbside.

"Airport, and fast," he growled in Batanian as they stepped hurriedly aboard.

"How are we going to pay him?" Steve whispered anxiously. "We haven't any Batanian money."

To his astonishment, Greg unfolded a roll of Batanian notes. "Took 'em out of Bell's pocket before I carried him from the cabin," Greg replied briefly. "Figured we might need some local currency. He'll get repaid in English cash when we get him out of Batania," he added, with grim determination.

At the airport they made their way to the arrival lounge. Planes were landing, but they carried only Batanians returning to their native country. No foreigners were permitted to enter since ZARB had seized control.

"How are we going to tell which are ZARB's secret agents?" Steve said under his breath.

The same thought had already occurred to Greg. Outside a line of vehicles awaited air travellers. Carefully Greg scrutinised them. Finally his gaze fastened on a large mini-bus. Beside the driver sat an armed soldier.

"My guess is that the mini-bus is waiting for 'em," he breathed. "They'll be coming in by several different planes, so we'll keep an eye on the bus and try to figure out if there's anything to distinguish ZARB's agents from other people."

Gradually the waiting bus began to fill as planes landed and their passengers disembarked, passing through the arrival lounge on their way out of the airport.

"Got it," Greg breathed at last. "Five men have gone aboard that mini-bus so far, after having first been met in the arrival lounge. Each one was wearing a glove on his right hand and carrying the other in his left. Steve, that must be the recognition sign."

As he spoke, Greg was already leaving the arrival lounge and heading for the passageway which led into it from the tarmac. The plane arrivals had to pass through this passage to reach the lounge. At its far end the door was open. Just inside the entrance was a closed door on which was a sign in Batanian, reading "Maintenance Store."

"See what's in here," Greg hissed and whipped open the door. It was a small room lined with buckets, brooms and cleaning equipment. "Excellent," he breathed shutting the door hurriedly and stepping back into the passage.

Greg and Steve waited on the tarmac. Another plane had landed, its passengers making their way towards the passage leading to the arrival lounge. Greg's eyes glinted. Two of the men were carrying gloves in their left hands and wearing gloves on their right. They were ZARB agents.

Boldly Greg stepped in front of the two men, making an urgent sign to them to step aside from the other passengers. They halted, eyeing him sharply, and this gave sufficient time for the others to vanish along the passage.

"Follow me," Greg rasped harshly. "We have transport to take you to the castle. ZARB waits there."

His sharp words and his air of authority convinced them. Without hesitation they followed him through the door into the pasage. Steve was waiting. Abruptly, he pushed wide the door to the maintenance room and with a violent shove, Greg hurled them into it.

The two spun round, each reaching for a hidden gun; but in a flash Greg and Steve were on them, bunched fists crashing into their jaws, hurling them backwards. Before

They were hurled backwards to the floor.

they could recover, the two daring under-cover agents had them covered with their own weapons.

"Okay," Greg rapped. "Strip off your raincoats and those gloves. We'll have your hats too."

It took only minutes for Greg and Steve to bind and gag the pair with their own hand-kerchiefs and braces and thrust them out of sight behind a pile of sacks and buckets.

"Into a raincoat, Steve, pull your hat well down over your face, put on one right glove, carry the other in your left hand and —we are two of ZARB's secret agents," Greg chuckled triumphantly. "Okay, this is where we stick our necks well and truly out."

"What do we do now?" Steve asked eagerly.

"We're going to take their places aboard that mini-bus," came the prompt reply. "Let's see what happens when we walk into the arrival lounge."

With their hats pulled low over their eyes they strode into the arrival lounge. Instantly a sharp-eyed man came towards them, glanced briefly down at their gloves, then nodded for them to follow him.

No sooner were they aboard the mini-bus, which was now full of men dressed almost exactly as Greg and Steve—in belted rain-coats and low-brimmed hats—than it moved off.

No one spoke, each man's head was buried in his chest. This suited the two undercover agents admirably; it meant less risk of detection on the journey to the castle, ZARB's headquarters on the outskirts of Lonz.

The mini-bus with its full load ran smoothly up the steep slope to the draw-bridge, halted as the sentries checked the driver's pass, then rolled to a halt in the courtyard inside the castle's grim walls.

"Out," came a sharp command, and as the men climbed down: "please to follow me. His Excellency, ZARB, awaits your arrival."

Steve darted a glance at Greg from under the rim of his hat, but Greg did not see it. His gaze was fastened on the man waiting to lead them to ZARB. The man was staring at

Greg, and his eyes were popping wide, his mouth opening in astonishment as he recognised him.

He was the man who had trailed Greg from the hospital, the man who had telephoned to ZARB warning him that the two spies were in Lonz itself.

He was recovering from his startled amazement and his mouth was opening to bellow an order to the sentries.

In one more second, Greg and Steve would be prisoners of ZARB in the very heart of his headquarters.

Chapter Three

GREG AND STEVE were the last out of the
mini-bus and the others were already enter-
ing the castle doors.

ZARB's agent sucked in a harsh breath,
about to shout the alarm that the two spies
were right there, in the castle courtyard.

Like lightning Greg acted! He let out a
furious roar which swung all eyes in his
direction, leapt at the Batanian and swung
a terrific blow to his jaw.

"A spy," Greg yelled, pointing dramati-
cally to the man now lying stunned at his
feet. "Arrest him!"

His startling accusation brought the sentries crowding to stare down at the sprawled
figure. Greg stepped back as though to let
them sieze him, signalled quickly to Steve
and they both slipped hastily after the others
through the castle doorway.

The ZARB agents were following a castle
guard up a flight of stone stairs. Greg sped
after them and stealthily inserted a tiny
locator pin into the belt of the last man.

He made another silent signal to Steve as they reached a wide stone-floored landing. Letting the agents follow the ZARB guard, Greg and Steve slipped quietly aside into the shadows of a narrow, winding corridor.

"Listen!" Greg halted Steve. "The chap I slogged has recovered, judging from the row coming from the courtyard. Guess he's proved his identity to ZARB's guards. They'll be haring into the castle after us in a jiff."

They broke into a cautious run along the corridor, lit only by slit openings in the thick castle wall. The loud thud of boots reverberated up the stone stairs followed by a brief silence as the guards reached the broad stone landing.

"They're splitting up," Steve gasped. "Sounds as if some of 'em are dashing along this passage."

Greg and Steve reached the far end. A spiral stone stairway wound upwards. Greg took the steps two at a time, Steve behind him, both making little or no noise as they climbed.

"Hold it," Greg suddenly hissed, his head

cocked. " Thunder—we've got thugs after us from above as well as below."

They stood there with grim faces, listening to the nearing sounds of pursuit from both above and below. They were snared between the two converging parties. Greg jerked round, eyeing the window by which they had stopped.

It was narrow, but, Greg figured, just wide enough for them to climb through. He thrust out his head, noted the terrifying drop to the courtyard below, and eyed a stone ledge circling the wall and running level with the base of the window recess.

There was no time for thought or hesitation. The drumming of booted feet was coming nearer from both above and below. At any moment ZARB's armed killers would pound round the corner and they would be trapped.

Greg hauled himself on to the narrow window-ledge, slid out of the stone-framed opening and on to the narrow ledge. He inched along a little to allow Steve to follow.

" The wall curves out of sight of the window opening," he hissed sideways to

Steve. They both had their backs pressed flat against the wall and their feet splayed wide on the precarious ledge. "Edge along it."

Stealthily, fearing to move at more than a snail's pace, Greg and Steve worked their way along and out of sight of the window.

Far below in the courtyard stood ZARB's sentries. At the slightest noise they might raise their eyes and notice the two fugitives sidling along the wall high above.

Cautiously twisting his head, because any sudden movement might unbalance him and hurl him from the ledge, Greg looked up. "Battlements above us," he breathed from the side of his mouth. "But I don't think we can reach them."

Steve slowly turned his head and darted a glance past Greg. He sucked in a harsh breath at what he saw. The ledge ended abruptly a few feet farther along!

He flicked a quick look downwards and hastily raised his eyes again, his stomach muscles tensing. It needed only the slightest slip to hurl him to the courtyard. And down there, besides the sentries, a detachment of armed guards now moved about, still on the look-out for the two daring British spies!

If one of those guards chanced to glance up he would see the quarry they were hunting. One murderous burst from a sub-machine-gun, and their riddled bodies would plunge from the ledge. Steve repressed a shudder.

"Steve!" Steve's eyes swerved sideways to Greg. "We've got to get over the battlements before those thugs spot us!"

"Sure, but how?" Steve gulped. "We can't make it from this ledge. There's no room to turn, reach up and haul ourselves over."

"Listen!" Greg hissed. They heard the thud of feet halt inside the castle and the loud breathing of someone whose head had been thrust through the window which was hidden from them by the curve of the wall. The loud breathing stopped suddenly. "Fine," Greg whispered. "One of our hunters has peered out, can't see us on this ledge, and has raced on away from the window."

"How's that going to help us?" Steve gasped.

"We'll work our way back to the window, and try to reach the battlements from the sill."

Inch by inch they edged their way back along the narrow ledge, not daring to look down or make the slightest noise in case the guards below would hear. Steve reached the window and cautiously eased his body through it, dropping silently inside with a deep breath of relief. A moment later Greg was at his side.

"I'm going out on the sill again," Greg breathed. "This time, I shall face the wall, and stretch up to see if I can reach the battlement embrasure above it. If I can, then I'm going to try to pull myself up. You must wrap your arms round my legs, Steve, to keep me from swaying back. Here goes."

He took a deep breath, then climbed through the window again, but this time he went backwards. Steve gripped him round the waist and cautiously Greg rose to his feet, facing the wall. As he got to his full height, Steve's encircling arms slid down until he was holding Greg round the thighs.

Balanced on the sill now at his full height,

Greg reached up. He found that his fingers could just close over the edge of the battlement embrasure.

"Steve," he whispered. "I'm going to try to haul myself up by my fingers. As my feet leave the sill, slide your hands underneath them, and ease me up. You'll have to plant your feet squarely and brace yourself against the wall by pressing your knees against it to take the strain of my weight. Ready?"

"All set," Steve breathed through clenched teeth.

Greg's body gradually began to rise as with all his strength, his muscles straining, he pulled himself up by his hands. Steve released his grip of Greg's legs and thrust his hands under the soles of his shoes. Gently he pushed upwards.

"Okay!" The whisper came down to him. "I'm sliding over the top," and Greg's legs vanished from view.

"Right, Steve. Get out on the sill backwards, and be mighty careful. Raise yourself slowly upright and slide your hands up the wall to me. I'll pull you up."

Steve took a deep breath, eased himself on to the sill and carefully got to his feet, clutching the top ledge of the window as he came to his full height. Raising one hand, he felt Greg's firm grip. Letting go the edge of the window he raised his other hand. Greg's grasp closed round it, and almost without effort it seemed, he was drawn up and over the battlement.

Thirty seconds later the two perspiring undercover agents were regaining their breath and rubbing their strained and aching limbs. Steve took a swift peep over the battlements. He gulped. If any of ZARB's guards had seen them . . . he turned away, shuddering.

Greg was holding his watch to his ear.

"The locator pin I stuck in one of the agent's raincoats is giving its signal," he said, and Steve heard the low buzz from the micro-receiver.

Greg began to move across the flat roof, and with every step the low buzz grew more insistent. It led them to the far end of the battlemented roof.

"That agent must be just below us," Greg exclaimed in a low voice.

"That means," Steve breathed excitedly, "ZARB's agents are at the meeting which

54

he ordered them to come to from all over the world."

Greg striding to the battlements, cautiously poked his head between them and peered down.

"We're in luck," he whispered over his shoulder. "ZARB thinks there's no risk of eavesdroppers outside that room, because it's high above the moat. He's got one window slightly open."

He was hurriedly clipping a micro-microphone, the size of a small button, to a length of nylon thread. Cautiously he lowered it until it was suspended alongside the open window. It gently swayed in the breeze.

Greg put the micro-receiver inside his watch to his ear, and Steve pressed close to listen.

A voice full of power and ringing harshly with triumph, came through the micro-receiver.

"——and this map of the world," they heard, "shows by its pin-flags where each of you will operate at zero hour. At zero plus six hours I, ZARB, will strike. Within one week of zero hour Batanians will be the master-race of the central Continent."

A cheer greeted his last statement.

"And ZARB rules Batania," Greg and Steve heard the shout. "Long live ZARB."

"Excellency, ZARB, what about the two spies?"

The listening undercover agents tensed as they heard the question, waiting eagerly to hear ZARB's answer.

"We baited a trap to bring them here," and Greg shot a startled glance at Steve. "We seized their friend from a hospital and brought him to my headquarters. ZARB knew that this man's British friends would feel in honour bound to rescue him." He gave a sneering laugh.

"They are in my castle," and his voice was suddenly evil with cold rage. "They will be caught, and then both they and their companion will be executed."

Greg's thoughts flashed to Bell. As ZARB had just said, Bell was a prisoner somewhere in the castle. Whatever the risk to themselves, he must be rescued.

His thoughts were suddenly interrupted. From his micro-receiver came a snarling hiss and in a flash, Greg guessed that the micro-sized transmitting microphone had been seen. A hasty glance over the battlement confirmed this—the breeze had wafted it inside the window.

He felt a tug on the nylon thread, and the microphone was torn from the thread.

Greg spun round. A stone stairway led up from the castle on to the roof. Its sides were bordered by a low wall. Mid-way along the roof an ancient, twisted chimney stack rose to support a small group of chimneys.

Dragging off his ZARB raincoat as he ran, Greg sprinted to the stack and arranged it so that the tip of a sleeve and the bottom hem of the coat just showed round the end of the stack. He hurtled back to Steve and hastily pushed him to the floor of the roof against the outer wall of the staircase, on the side farthest from the stack.

With a rush a bunch of ZARB's toughest Batanian guards pounded up the stone stairway on to the roof.

" There, behind the chimney stack," came the cry, followed immediately by a thunderous chatter of gun-fire. Greg and Steve's ear-drums were almost shattered as the guards continued to direct a scorching hail of bullets at the stack and the coat.

As they fired, the guards, yelling viciously, raced towards the stack, intent on slaughter.

"Over the wall," Greg gritted and with lightning vaults both men hurtled down on to the stone stairway, throwing themselves recklessly to the narrow passageway at its foot.

From above, the echoing roar of sub-machine-guns drowned the drumming of their feet as Greg and Steve sped along the passageway.

Suddenly Greg snatched at Steve, dragging him to a halt!

An open doorway threw daylight into the passage. On tip-toe, Greg edged towards the door until he was able to steal a rapid glance round its post.

One lightning glimpse, and Greg knew he was looking into the heart of ZARB's headquarters. This was ZARB's inner sanctum, the room in which his schemes were planned and his orders despatched to his secret agents all over the world.

A huge desk was in its centre, surrounded by consoles of instruments and switches, television screens and microphones. On the desk was a battery of telephones.

On the far side of the room, at the window in front of which Greg had dangled his micro-transmitter, stood a group of men— ZARB's secret agents, those who had ridden in the mini-bus with Greg and Steve.

In their midst towered a massive, powerful figure, glaring at something in his huge palm. Greg guessed what it was—his captured mike!

Greg gave a sudden start of excitement.

A huge map of the world hung on one of the walls. Stuck in the map were small, coloured flags.

" By thunder," Greg breathed into Steve's ear, " that must be the map ZARB was babbling about just now to those agents crowding round him. The flags mark the places all over the world where these men are going to operate at ZARB's secret zero hour."

His fist flashed to a pocket. Steve saw him put what looked like a cigarette lighter to his eye and depress its trigger.

Inside the lighter was recorded on tape a pin-head size photograph of every detail of the huge map and its flags. When the microfilm was printed and enlarged to the same size as the map on ZARB's wall, the secret of his agents' operational spots would be revealed to Greg—and to WASP. But Greg had yet to discover what was ZARB's fearful plan.

Without warning ZARB, towering above the agents who surrounded him, spun round. His eyes flashed over their heads—and met those of Greg as he lowered his lighter-camera.

ZARB burst through the agents, scattering them as he dived to his massive desk and thrust a huge fist to a switch.

Greg leapt away from the door, dragging Steve clear and turned to race along the passage.

Crash! The door clanged shut and, clang-clang—steel shutters crashed down in front and behind them!

"He's got us boxed in," Steve gasped.

They were imprisoned between the stone wall of the passage on one side, the steel door of ZARB's room on the other, and steel shutters before and behind them.

Greg staggered. Steve let out a startled cry. The floor under them was moving side-ways, disappearing under the stone wall.

" Look," Steve choked, his eyes goggling as they fastened on the opening revealed by the steadily widening gap at their feet.

They were forced to use their feet as though walking. The floor was slowly, remorselessly going from under them in a steady movement, vanishing into a slit in the stone wall.

A black chasm was widening, its depths hidden in menacing darkness, and Greg knew its bottom lay far below in the dungeons under ZARB's castle.

In a few more seconds the last of the floor would have disappeared under the stone wall; and as it vanished, they would plunge to their deaths in that terrible black void.

Chapter Four

"Quick, Steve, plant your feet against the wall and jam your body against the opposite wall."

Greg was already forcing his body into a sitting position. With outstretched legs, he pressed his feet rigidly against the far wall and thrust his back hard against the one facing it.

Steve copied Greg just as the last of the floor vanished from sight. He held his breath as his gaze flashed under his outstretched body. A fearful black chasm yawned below. He could see no bottom—it was hidden in darkness.

"Can't stick it—for long," he gasped. Greg saw that Steve's feet were beginning to slip in spite of his desperate attempts to keep them pressed against the wall facing him.

Greg suddenly opened his mouth and let out a howling shriek. It roared wildly, then rapidly faded into silence. Steve gulped.

It was a horrible sound, like a man hurtling into space and falling to his death.

Tensely Greg waited. Would his trick work? Would ZARB have heard that awful yell fade away to sudden silence? Would he believe the spy with the camera had plunged to his death far below?

The floor reappeared, sliding from under the wall, closing over the terrible gap.

Muscles were at breaking point as they slid to the floor and sucked in great lungfuls of air. Greg flashed to his feet. The shutters were sweeping up. In a moment the door to ZARB's HQ would open.

"Get going," he hissed, and with Steve racing after him, Greg sped along the passage. Behind them they heard ZARB's roof-searching thugs running down the stone steps at the other end of the passage.

Light bulbs illuminated the passage, a tough electric cable linking the lights. Greg halted and with a lightning snip of his insulated clippers cut through the cable, leaving the passage in almost total darkness.

"Won't spot us when they reach the passage from the roof," he rapped, racing on along the seemingly endless passage and desperately hunting for an escape from it.

At last a low door appeared in the outer wall. Greg wrenched back a bolt and burst it open. Beyond was a small circular room with deep-set window spaces round its outer wall.

"A curtain tower," Greg rapped darting to one of the unglazed window openings and jutting his head through it. "Steve, look below."

The curtain tower projected from a corner of the castle wall. Steve looked down. His eyes gleamed. In a small enclosed courtyard stood the ambulance which had brought the kidnapped Bell to the castle.

Hastily Greg calculated the distance to the cobbled courtyard. About thirty feet!

He abruptly withdrew his head and leapt to the door, closing it quietly and quickly. Hurrying footsteps were echoing along the passage. The two tensed, then relaxed as the steps pounded past the door.

"ZARB's thugs going down to the dungeons, expecting to find our bodies," Greg muttered. "ZARB must have commanded 'em to recover my secret camera."

"Phee-ew!" Steve's expression was grim.

With a lightning snip he cut through the cable.

"When they fail to find said bodies they'll start a search for us—this time they'll comb the castle from top to bottom."

"Right," Greg rapped. "So we can't hide out in this curtain tower; and to attempt to sneak back either along the passage or elsewhere is too risky. There's only one way out of this tower."

Without explaining what he meant, Greg prised open the door and peered cautiously along the corridor which, without electric light, was like a long, dim vault.

It was empty. Creeping out, he sped along until he reached the place where he had cut through the cable. Gripping its loose end, Greg wrenched at the cable. His tug pulled the cable-pins from the wall. He then tore the other end from the overhead light fitting and dashed back to the curtain tower.

Steve watched Greg expertly loop one end of the cable to the centre post of a window space and drop the remainder from the window. A quick look told him that it almost reached the cobbles.

"Shin down, Steve," Greg said. "Watch

your palms. Don't slide, or you'll skin 'em. Go down hand over hand."

He watched Steve go skilfully down the tough cable and drop the last few feet to the courtyard. Steve waved up and Greg followed quickly, hand over hand.

He darted to the ambulance. It was empty, as he expected—and feared. So Bell was a prisoner in the castle just as ZARB had boasted.

As long as Bell was alive, there was the hope that when he recovered from the blow on his head, he would remember the secret of ZARB's plans. It was vital that they rescue him and learn the nature of those plans. But ZARB had spoken of zero hour —unless they could find and snatch Bell from ZARB's clutches and all three make their escape before then, their mission would have failed. And the consequences of that failure might be disastrous for the whole world!

There was a low, iron-studded door in the wall. Greg gently turned its massive ring-handle. It lifted an inner latch but the door remained fast. It had no lock and Greg knew it must be double bolted inside—a formidable and almost impossible barrier to overcome.

Greg whipped from his nylon thigh-case a tiny nozzle-head, a short length of steel tube and a cigarette-size cylinder. He screwed the nozzle to one end of the tube, the cylinder to the other.

Giving the cylinder a half-turn, he sparked his lighter at the nozzle. A six-inch white-hot flame, almost invisible so fierce was its intensity, hissed from the nozzle.

"Keep guard," Greg grunted, bending to his task of slicing through the metal of the door.

Steve crouched down watching Greg and at the same time on the alert for the sound of anyone approaching the outer gate of the courtyard. The super-cutting flame raced through the iron door and Greg directed it on to a bolt on the inner side.

"Bolt one gone," he muttered, and two minutes later, "bolt two. Let's try that latch again!"

The door swung open with a groan of heavy hinges. They crept over the threshhold and paused, listening.

"We're in the kitchens of the castle," Steve whispered, and Greg nodded. "That door, Greg. Looks as if it leads down below. Dungeons, I'd guess."

"And that's probably where Bell is," Greg growled. "We'll investigate 'em."

They tip-toed across the huge stone-floored kitchen and carefully opened the door. Beside it were two large rubber dustbins full of garbage. That meant the kitchens were in frequent use but, luckily for them, not at this moment.

Both froze! From below had come a shout.

"They're not down here. We've searched the dungeons. They've succeeded in escaping ZARB's trap. Warn ZARB."

"Wow," and Steve gave a brief grin at Greg. "ZARB's thugs have discovered there aren't any bodies down there."

Distantly they heard a voice shouting into an internal telephone, reporting to ZARB. Both spun round, eyeing a loudspeaker on the kitchen wall. From it boomed a powerful voice, and it was icy with menace.

"ZARB to all personnel. Switch on your nerve-controls. Repeat, switch on your nerve-controls. Stand by for count-down. Beginning now. Ten—nine——" the voice thundered on counting backwards until, "two—one—zero!"

Steve gave a mighty shiver. His eyes jerked to Greg. Greg was shivering as though he was being shaken from head to foot by a terrible fever. Steve felt his own body shaking faster and faster until his arms, legs, and head seemed about to burst away from his trunk.

He could hardly breathe, his throat was closing up, or so it seemed. His head was quaking and shaking so violently that he could not focus his eyes on Greg.

Greg's legs were buckling under him; his whole frame seemed to be in the power of a terrible, invisible control which was rapidly reducing him to utter helplessness. His brain was dazed; but Greg knew that unless he could overcome this awful power, both he and Steve could not survive the body-shattering vibrations many more minutes.

Calling upon all his reserves of stamina, Greg overturned one of the two rubber dust-bins, spilling its garbage to the floor. Then pushing the almost unconscious Steve under the dustbin, he upturned it over him.

Greg was almost on the point of passing out. Barely able to see, unable to suck breath into his empty lungs, the intensity of the vibrations was shaking the last ounces of strength out of him. But with a last frenzied effort, he overturned the second rubber bin, fell to the floor and pulled it upside down over himself.

Instantly his violent shaking and shivering stopped. He gulped, sucked and swallowed great gusts of air, foul though it was under the garbage bin, and strength poured back into his limbs and his head began to clear.

"If it wasn't for the rubber bins," he gasped to himself, "Steve and I would both be goners! The rubber is insulating us from ZARB's murderous nerve machine. His order to his thugs must have been to switch on some sort of anti-nerve vibrator that each must carry."

In the darkness of the inverted bin, he peered at his luminous watch. He would give it a full minute, then raise the rubber shelter which had saved his life.

The seconds crept on. When the minute was up, Greg cautiously lifted the edge of the bin. He felt nothing, and slowly he raised it further. Steve was still concealed under his rubber shelter. Greg pushing his bin clear, rose to his feet and lifted up Steve's covering.

"ZARB's switched off his killer," he said briefly. "Figures it must have done its work, and reckons that by now we've both been vibrated to death. No one could survive it for more than a few moments."

Below, beyond the foot of the stone steps leading to the dungeons they could hear footsteps retreating on the cobbled flooring. Greg made a sign to Steve to follow and silently he crept down the steps.

Both suddenly halted. ZARB's voice was again booming through loudspeakers somewhere in the dungeons.

"The two agents are now dead!" he announced. "Search for and find their bodies. On one is a secret micro-camera in the form of a cigarette lighter. Recover and bring. Repeat—recover and bring. This is top priority."

Greg breathed, "ZARB must have the

whole castle wired, Steve, m'lad. All the wiring must be stapled to the stonework and not buried in the walls—they're too tough."

Steve nodded, wondering what shrewd plan was passing through Greg's quick brain. He did not have to wait long to find out what it was. Greg was checking the walls for electric cables, using them as signposts in a determined search for Bell.

"Wherever they have Bell imprisoned down here, there is certain to be electric light, so that his jailers can spy on him through a peep-hole in the door," Greg whispered in a confident tone.

Steve was sure Greg was right and, anyway, he could not think of any better lead to follow. The dungeons appeared to be vast, with a maze of dank, dark passages, some lighted by overhead bulbs, others pitch dark.

Greg ignored the unlit passages, tracking only those with cable pinned along the walls. They stole past grim, shadowy recesses, dank and evil-smelling caves of darkness which they knew had, at one time, been the life-long prisons of chained captives.

Greg suddenly stopped and eyed a junction box which was screwed to the wall above a closed door. The cable leading to the junction box was a power cable. His eyes glinted.

"There's something more than electric light on the other side of this door," he said in a low voice.

Without making a sound, he slowly turned the door handle. To his surprise, the door gave. It swung open soundlessly.

They both tensed!

Two men in short-sleeved white smocks and white trousers stooped over a figure strapped on one of two couches. Both men wore medical masks which hid all but their eyes.

The man on the bed was Bell! His eyes were open, staring defiantly at the two doctors bending over him. One of them held a hypodermic syringe poised above Bell's arm; he was about to plunge in the needle.

"Now that he's conscious, this will make him tell all he knows," Greg heard him say. "He's still weak and dazed, but this truth drug will force him to speak. ZARB fears that this man knows his secret plan—and zero hour. If he does, he will reveal his knowledge when I jab this needle into him."

Steve's teeth clenched in cold rage. Before Greg could make an attempt to stop him, Steve had leapt past him through the open doorway to throw himself on the doctor with the syringe.

In mid-flight Steve suddenly halted. Greg, hidden from the eyes of the two doctors who had spun round at the sound of Steve's rush, saw his friend stiffen like a stone statue.

Steve was poised on one foot, the other in mid-air, in a running position. One arm was outstretched, its fist clenched, the other half-raised, ready to follow through with a mighty body slam.

He was immobilised, held captive, unable to move, not even to bat his eyelids, by some mysterious, unseen force. Greg, gaping at him, knew that Steve was gripped by a radiated power flooding between the door posts, a power which was ZARB's invisible sentinel.

"One of the two foreign agents!" he heard one of the doctors gloat excitedly. "Trapped by the guardian ray. He may be the one with the secret camera. Somehow he has survived ZARB's nerve-destroying vibrator."

Greg backed hastily out of sight, flattening himself in the shadow of a buttress as the two white-uniformed men crossed to the door. Greg heard a switch being thrown and the sound of Steve instantly reviving and continuing his rush into the room.

"They've switched off their guardian ray," Greg gritted under his breath.

He stole to the open door and darted a fleeting glance round its post. One of the two men had Steve covered with a gun while the other was strapping him to the second couch, alongside Bell.

He saw Steve being searched swiftly and expertly. In a few minutes, the doctors stepped back, fuming. One of them strode to an intercom phone.

"Excellency ZARB," he rasped savagely. "We have one of the two enemy spies. He does not have secret camera. He survived your vibrator death. Other spy most probably still alive. Your orders, Excellency ZARB."

Greg heard a shout of rage boom from the intercom, then, over the loudspeakers ZARB roared a command.

"Don masks, repeat, masks—immediately. Stand by. Enemy agent in castle. This time he will die. All vapour controls being opened. Vapour on—NOW."

A faint hissing broke from somewhere nearby. Greg, in the shadow of the buttress, shot an uneasy glance upwards along the passage. He could see nothing, but the hissing was increasing in volume.

A furious desire to cough gripped him. He choked it back. The doctors would hear it. His eyes began to sting, his throat burned, his breathing was difficult, he felt dizzy.

"Killer gas," he thought dazedly. "ZARB has turned on an invisible vapour to kill me."

He knew he was about to drift into unconsciousness—and death. Without a gas mask he stood no chance of surviving ZARB's murderous killer vapour.

Vapour! His brain, struggling against the darkness stealing over it, registered the word. Vapour—lighter than air . . . floats upwards. Vapour—up—air—below!

He slid to the floor. He had all but passed out, yet his tremendous will-power forced him to struggle to turn his body over, rolling his lips to the cold stone floor. A draught of untainted air swept into his gasping lungs and with it a surge of power gripped him.

Greg's desperate last-second action had saved his life. The air at floor-level was free of the light, poisonous vapour floating above it.

His thoughts flashed to ZARB with a cold, icy hatred. The inhuman monster and his vile evil scheme, whatever it was, had to be destroyed to save the peace of the world.

Flat on the floor, he crawled swiftly back to the open doorway and peered round it. The two white-coated villains were again stooping over Bell; the syringe was again about to be plunged into him.

Greg flashed a hand over the threshold. Nothing happened. He thrilled with joy. In their excitement the pair had omitted to switch on the guardian ray.

He rose to his feet, took a small glass ball from his nylon thigh case and hurled it

A draught of air swept into his lungs . . .

across the room at the fuse box on the far wall. As the glass shattered, a brilliant red flash burst from the fuse box.

The two doctors spun round, one of them crying out "Fuse box is short-circuiting. Quick, switch it off before everything is burnt out."

The pair raced towards the fuse box. Greg flashed across the room and dived under the couch to which Steve was strapped. With his sheath knife he slashed through the straps.

"You're free, Steve," he whispered, and as the two doctors returned to continue their work on Bell, Steve suddenly leapt from his couch while Greg shot to his feet from beneath it.

Before the two men in white knew what was happening, Greg and Steve were upon them with bunched fists flying. Within seconds the two doctors lay unconscious.

Greg leapt to Bell and unstrapped him. Steve suddenly hissed a warning. A crowd of men were hurrying along the passageway. Greg's eyes flashed round the room, then he pointed to a heavy wooden door set deep in the far wall.

"What's in there?" he hissed, and Steve

raced to it, pulling at the door. It creaked open revealing a gloomy, shallow recess—a long-disused store cupboard. " Get Bell in there, quickly," rapped Greg urgently.

Steve gripped Bell, who staggered dazedly, and pulled him into the cupboard. Hastily Steve shut the door and dashed back to Greg who was stripping the two stunned doctors of their white smocks and trousers.

At a sign from Greg, Steve pulled on a short-sleeved smock and white trousers while Greg swiftly did likewise. The footsteps were almost at the door.

There was no time to dress the two men in their own clothes. Greg snatched two oxygen masks, clapped them on the faces of the unconscious men then quickly lifted them on to the couches.

" Hide your face with a medical mask," Greg hissed to Steve, and just as they finished tying the tapes behind their heads, into the room strode ZARB, followed by a squad of his thugs, each armed with a sub-machine-gun.

ZARB strode to the foot of the two couches, his eyes raking the two figures and fastening finally on the oxygen masks which covered their faces. Greg and Steve behind their medical masks watched him grimly, tense and alert. What would ZARB do now?

Abruptly ZARB swung round to Greg, his eyes boring into him as though he would read what lay behind the concealing medical mask.

"Has the truth drug revealed his secret?" he thundered, pointing at first one, then the other masked figure lying on the couches.

Greg's pulses thumped. Would his voice betray him if he answered ZARB? He could speak the language almost as well as a native, but it was possible that ZARB knew the doctor well enough to recognise his voice.

There was no time to hesitate. ZARB's deep-set eyes were fixed on Greg. He wanted an instant answer.

From behind his mask Greg put a harsh snarl into his voice, making it appear to ring with frustrated fury. He hoped it would fool ZARB.

"The truth drug produced nothing," he

snarled, "and that is because he can know nothing of your secret plans, Excellency ZARB."

Steve listened in silent admiration. Greg had spoken the truth. The drug had produced nothing, because he and Greg had prevented its use; and it was unlikely that either of the two unconscious doctors would know ZARB's secret plans.

They saw ZARB's face gleam with silent satisfaction. His fear that the kidnapped secret agent knew his secret was unfounded.

"There is still the other enemy spy," he boomed in a murderous voice. "My vapour should have dealt with him. His body and his secret camera will be found. So—now my secret plans are safe."

He threw a brief look of hate at the two figures on the couches then pointed at Greg and Steve.

"I want these two enemy agents killed."

He paused, his eyes roaming round the room, halting as he stared at a high-voltage incinerator. A cruel, evil expression crossed his face. His lips curled viciously.

"You two doctors," he rasped loudly,

" lift the two spies into that incinerator and destroy them completely. Burn them to ashes. NOW. I will watch."

And he stepped back, waiting for Greg and Steve to wheel the couches to the incinerator, lift the two unconscious figures into it, and switch on the high-voltage current!

Behind ZARB, his armed thugs grinned evilly, ready to threaten the two men in medical masks if they hesitated to carry out ZARB's terrible order.

Chapter Five

GREG MUST SHOW no hesitation. ZARB was watching his every movement, and the armed thugs who were part of ZARB's army would be only too happy to drill him and Steve, if either made the smallest attempt to escape.

Besides, Bell was concealed in the cupboard. In addition to saving themselves, they had also to rescue Bell. He had, at long last, recovered consciousness and it was imperative that they should as soon as possible learn from him ZARB's fearful plan and ZARB's zero hour.

"Must check the controls, Excellency ZARB," Greg stated in a steady, cool voice and crossed the floor to the thick wooden door of the cupboard. If he could open it partly, keeping his body between the watching ZARB and his thugs, he could pretend that he was making a rapid check of a control panel inside the cupboard.

His real purpose was to hiss a warning

to Bell—to be ready for whatever action Greg might take to outwit ZARB in a desperate attempt to escape.

Opening the door slightly, he looked round.

Greg all but let out a startled cry!

Bell was not in the cupboard! He had disappeared!

With an effort, he forced himself to remain calm and look casual as he closed the door and turned to rejoin Steve. ZARB bellowed suddenly at him.

"You waste time. One minute I give. Put spies in incinerator and kill—or I have you both shot."

"Push the couches over to the incinerator," Greg breathed to Steve through his medical mask.

The pair trundled the laden couches alongside the massive incinerator. Greg flashed a quick glance from them to the cupboard, measuring the floor distance. ZARB was watching his every move through narrowed eyes.

"ZARB's beginning to suspect something's wrong," Steve murmured, just loud enough for Greg to hear.

Steve was right. The ruthless dictator's

brow was creased as he stared at the two figures on the couches. Something about them was suddenly stirring his suspicions. Abruptly he strode across the floor towards them.

In another second he would reach the couches. He had only to strip the oxygen masks from the faces of the two men lying there to learn the truth.

Greg remained quite calm. Appearing not to notice ZARB's sudden movement he reached up to the incinerator as though to switch on its power.

But concealed in his palm, was his pair of insulated wire clippers. A lightning snick and he had cut the power cable. Gripping one end of the cut cable with the clippers, he let it brush against the steel incinerator.

One brief flash—and the fuses exploded, plunging the room into utter darkness.

Greg stooped and gave one of the couches a mighty push, sending it shooting across the blacked-out room towards the unseen figure of ZARB. The other couch he thrust towards ZARB's guards who were now yelling furiously.

Crashes, shouts and moans filled the darkness as Greg grabbed Steve's wrist and steered him to the cupboard. Opening the door, he bundled Steve inside and following quickly, shut the door behind him.

"There must be a secret door, otherwise how did Bell vanish from inside this ancient cupboard?" Greg muttered, as he flashed his pencil torch over the brick walls.

He could see no sign of a hidden exit. Outside the cupboard ZARB was roaring for torches. Greg knew he had only a few desperate seconds before the armed men in the room would burst open the cupboard and find them.

He ran his fingers over the brickwork, seeking a hidden pressure point, a knob, anything that would open the secret door that must be there. His probing fingers found nothing. Steve watched in grim anxiety.

"Bell couldn't have known there was a secret exit when you pushed him in here," Greg hurriedly whispered. "He must have found it by accident. What would he have done when he was shut up in total darkness in the cupboard?"

Bell had still been dazed, uncertain on his feet. "He would almost certainly have leaned against the wall to support himself!" Steve whispered.

The wall! Yes, but which one? When Steve had thrust him in and shut the door, Bell would no doubt have staggered to the wall farthest from the door, and it would most likely have been his shoulder which came in contact with the wall.

Thinking thus at jet speed, Greg focused his pencil-beam torch on the brickwork in the far wall at what he calculated to be Bell's shoulder height. Steadily, in spite of the rising clamour outside the cupboard, he pressed each brick in turn across the width of the wall.

"They've got the lights on again," gasped Steve suddenly. "ZARB's killers will burst the door open any minute."

Greg's jaw clenched hard. His pressure on the bricks had no result. From outside they heard ZARB roar.

"Search that cupboard!"

In desperation Greg swept the torch beam up and down the wall. Suddenly Steve heard him utter a hiss. Near the foot of the wall a cobweb was broken. Greg had no time to stoop to press there. Raising his foot, he kicked the wall just where the cobweb had been.

Behind them the wall swung slowly open.

In a flash Greg was thrusting Steve through the widening gap and pushing after him. Turning, he put his shoulder to the rear of the wall and thrust it back into place.

As the wall closed behind them they could hear faintly the noise of the cupboard door being burst open. Then a bellow reached them.

" They were in here. Look !"

Greg flashed the torch into Steve's face. His medical mask no longer covered it. It must have fallen off in the cupboard. ZARB's armed guards had just found it.

" Bell's shoe must accidentally have kicked the secret lever which opened the wall at the back of the cupboard and he fell through," Greg gritted. He was flashing his torch as he spoke. A low-roofed, dank passage wound ahead.

" Yes, but where is he ?" Steve snapped.

" Must have staggered along this passage," came the swift retort. " Probably still so dazed he didn't know what he was doing. Listen!" And he threw a sharp glance backwards. "Those thugs know that somehow we've escaped through the back of that cupboard wall. They are trying to smash down the brickwork."

Heavy blows echoed through the passage as they stumbled along it. Greg was leading, when Steve heard him utter a sharp warning to halt.

Bell lay on the damp floor, panting and only half-conscious. Hurriedly Greg stooped and picking him up, hoisted him over a shoulder, then struggled on under the low roof of the seemingly endless passage.

A shattering roar from behind, followed by a rush of air along the passage told Greg and Steve what had happened. ZARB's men had blown open the brick wall. Yells echoed menacingly. The armed soldiers were now pursuing them along the passage.

"Greg, its light ahead!"

Greg had already seen it. The darkness was thinning and as they rounded a bend, dim daylight flooded the end of the passage.

Quickening their steps, they made all the

speed they could towards it. Suddenly Greg, who was in the lead, with Bell on his shoulder, came to a halt.

Steve let out a groan of dismay!

The long, winding passage ended at the foot of a shaft. Looking up, they could see daylight, about fifteen feet above them.

Greg lowered Bell to the floor of the shaft. Even by standing on Steve's shoulders, he could not hope to reach the lip of the shaft; but without hesitation Greg planted a foot against one wall, both hands against the opposite wall and began to force himself up the shaft—walking up the wall.

He was an experienced rock climber and this narrow shaft was no more difficult for Greg than some of the natural chimneys he had climbed.

Steve strained his head backwards and watched anxiously, while at the same time his ears were cocked listening to the triumphant yells from far down the passage. Their pursuers were hard on their heels.

Sweat streamed from Greg as, at last, he hauled himself over the lip of the shaft. He wiped it out of his eyes and Steve saw him give an excited wave down the shaft.

" Steve, I'm in the courtyard alongside the ambulance. It's right here. Stand by, I'm going to lower a stretcher. Strap Bell to it."

Steve reached up and grasped the end of the stretcher. The shaft was too narrow to lay it flat. Propping it against the wall, he lifted Bell and rested him against the stretcher, then strapped him securely to it.

Gasping under its weight Steve thrust it upwards. Greg leaned over, reached down and just succeeded in reaching the stretcher. With a mighty pull he hauled it over and out of the shaft.

" Greg!" Steve's loud and alarmed cry brought Greg to the shaft to peer down anxiously. " ZARB's men are nearly here!"

Like lightning Greg unstrapped Bell, tore back to the shaft and lowered the stretcher.

" Hang on to it," he called down. " I'm going to haul you up."

Straining every muscle he heaved, and gradually Steve, clinging grimly to the stretcher, was raised to the top of the air shaft. With a final shoulder-wrenching pull Greg hauled him over.

" Get Bell into the ambulance," he panted.

" ZARB's lads will be bursting into this courtyard just as soon as they discover they can't get up that shaft."

Steve carried Bell to the ambulance and pushed him inside. Bell had partly recovered but was still dazed. Meantime Greg had reached the cab of the ambulance and had climbed into the driving-seat.

He depressed the starter and it answered at once to his touch. Breathing more easily, Greg steered the vehicle across the yard, slowing as he reached its closed gate.

He was about to leap down to open it when—Wha-am! Crash! The windscreen splintered into a thousand tiny criss-cross lines. Greg's teeth clenched. An unseen sniper had the ambulance in his sights. His shot had made the windscreen a mass of fractured glass through which he could see nothing.

Greg did not hesitate. Bunching a fist he smashed it through the glass, making a large hole. A sentry, his rifle to his shoulder had rushed round a corner and was about to take another shot.

Greg took his foot off the brake, let in the clutch and stamped on the accelerator. The ambulance leapt forward straight at the closed gate, sweeping the sentry aside and knocking the rifle out of his grip.

The heavy bonnet charged into the timber of the gate. The noise of splintering wood screeched along both sides of the ambulance as the vehicle crashed through the shattered gate. Out across the main courtyard it tore and on towards the bridge over the moat.

ZARB's guards spun round as the ambulance bounded over the cobbles with fragments of the wrecked gate clinging to its bonnet and wings.

"Close the bridge," one of the guards bellowed and Greg glimpsed through the hole in the windscreen a sentry leaping to the control button which would winch up the bridge.

He swung the wheel. With tyres screaming, the ambulance lurched wildly, but thanks to Greg's skilful steering, righted itself and the vehicle charged straight towards the buttress on which the control button was located.

The guard, about to press the button, shrieked in terror as the massive bonnet raced at him as though it was about to pinion him against the stone buttress. He hurled himself clear and ran for his life.

Greg spun the wheel again. The ambulance brushed the buttress, shattering a side window as it went. The tyres skimmed the base of the wall, then Greg was driving furiously under the portcullis and over the drawbridge, scattering the sentries before they could empty their sub-machine-guns into the ambulance.

The vehicle rocked from side to side, as with foot hard down on the accelerator, and crouching low over the wheel, Greg hurled the vehicle off the bridge on to the road.

"Going to make a dash for the border through the mountains," he yelled over his shoulder. Steve and Bell, clutching stretcher rests in the back of the ambulance to avoid being hurled to the floor, just nodded.

The wheels pounded along the winding road which now began to climb. Greg knew that already ZARB would have taken desperate steps to prevent their escape from Batania. He dared not let Bell cross the frontier for fear of what he might know about the mysterious and terrible plan.

"No sign of pursuit, Greg," Steve shouted,

after a long scrutiny of the road rolling away behind them.

Greg nodded, his eyes fixed on the road ahead. They were now in the foothills and were steadily climbing at the fastest speed which Greg could get out of the machine. They topped a long, steep rise.

"Viaduct," he bellowed. "Crosses a rail track. Can't see any guards . . ."

He broke off. Suddenly from behind a peak a helicopter had appeared, and it was coming straight for the road along which the ambulance was thundering.

"By heck, it's going to attack us!"

Greg muttered the warning but Steve had already seen the flash of gunfire from the helicopter. He glanced at Bell and was relieved to see that he now seemed to have fully recovered from the fearful blow on his head.

"Okay, Steve," he exclaimed, his voice firm. "I'm all right, now. That chopper is figuring on knocking out this ambulance before it can cross the viaduct."

"Guess so," Steve grimly agreed. "ZARB must have radioed the pilot to ambush us on the bridge."

The helicopter zoomed nose down on the ambulance, its gun spitting savagely. Greg watched it narrowly, and as the chopper roared head-on and less than fifty feet above the viaduct, Greg accelerated to top speed, shot beneath it, braked furiously and stopped.

"Out," he yelled over his shoulder, while the pilot of the chopper swung his machine in a tight circle to repeat his attack.

Steve and Bell leapt from the rear of the ambulance and dashed after Greg who was already climbing over the viaduct rails and down the wooden supports beneath it.

"Climb under the bridge," Greg ordered. "That chopper pilot can't get at us there."

In desperate haste they edged under the span of the long wooden bridge. Steve eyed the structure contemptuously as they crouched.

"Look at those upright supports," Steve growled. "Don't look strong enough to hold up the bridge. No British engineer would produce such a bad job. The supports are no thicker than gate posts."

Greg heard but did not reply. His gaze

*The helicopter zoomed down on the
ambulance . . .*

was fixed on a pair of booted feet which had suddenly appeared below the bridge span. They swayed in a rope sling which was dropping lower and lower until the figure of a man in the uniform of ZARB's air force swung into view.

The man was strapped to a cable attached to the helicopter which was now hovering above and to one side of the viaduct. He was clutching a Sterling sub-machine-gun!

He caught sight of Greg, Steve and Bell crouching under the shelter of the viaduct. They saw him give a swift wave to the pilot. The cable steadied, he turned in his sling and the sub-machine-gun swung round until it was pointing at the three fugitives.

A burst of fire crashed with shattering echoes, and splinters of bullet-ripped timbers tore the air round them.

"Missed that time," Greg gasped. "But if he can steady the swing of that cable he's going to make mincemeat of us with his next burst."

And as he spoke, they saw the cable being turned by the winch-control which was out of their sight.

The machine-gunner was again taking

aim and Greg knew that this time he would send a volley, fanning it to and fro to make sure of sending a murderous shower of lead into the three British agents.

The gunner's lips were parted in savage triumph.

He had them trapped.

Chapter Six

GREG'S EYES flashed away from the cable and the machine-gunner. They darted to the bullet-riddled woodwork, and with a speed that was so fast that Steve almost missed Greg's action, he tore a splintered chunk of timber from its nailed fixture.

He hurled it, whizzing and twisting at catapult force. The torn chunk smashed against the enemy's jaw. The man sagged senseless on the cable, his sub-machine-gun slipping from his grasp!

Greg took a flying leap towards the cable —and the falling weapon.

One fist snatched at the cable, the other at the sub-machine-gun already sliding free and about to fall to the rail-track below.

"He's got it!" Steve yelled in excitement, and Greg, breathing hard, swung the cable towards the bridge uprights, released his grip and let his body hurtle to the supports, grabbing at them with his free hand.

The stunned gunner was being winched out of sight by the helicopter. Greg was thinking furiously. They must get Bell across the frontier. Bell knew ZARB's secret and he himself had a camera record of the huge map and its mysterious flags.

The beat of the helicopter's rotor was fading. Steve grinned at Greg. The pilot had given up! He had no chance against them with the viaduct above acting as a shield.

"Climb back up top," Greg commanded when the thrum of the machine had finally died away. "Get aboard the ambulance again, if the chopper hasn't blown its engine to pieces. We've got to make a dash for the frontier before ZARB's killers close in on us."

He swung over the parapet on to the bridge. Steve and Bell, about to follow, heard him yell a brief warning.

"Stay below! The ambulance is knocked out; and an armoured car is racing towards the viaduct."

His last words were almost lost to them as a brisk rat-a-tat-tat of rapid fire burst from the armoured car tearing down the slope to the viaduct.

Greg leapt for his life, vaulting over the

rails, still clutching the sub-machine-gun in one hand while with the other he held on to the supports and swung himself back under the bridge.

Crouching between the uprights, he trained the muzzle of the weapon on the supports under one end of the viaduct. They could hear the armoured car tearing down the hill, about to thunder on to the wooden planking of the bridge.

Greg squeezed the trigger. A blazing swathe of lead cut into the upright supports at the speed of five hundred shots a minute. Steve thrilled with excitement.

It was as though a buzz-saw was ripping through the wood and slashing cleanly through every one of the timbers.

As suddenly as the sub-machine-gun had roared into thunderous action, it ceased. Its magazine was emptied. Now useless, Greg hurled the weapon aside and saw it spin to the rail-track below.

"Listen," Steve cried. "That armoured car is about to sweep on to the viaduct." The three tensed expectantly.

The planking suddenly shuddered as the

weighty armoured car rumbled from the sloping road on to the bridge.

Gripping uprights half-way along the bridge's supports the three men waited grimly.

As the heavy machine rolled over the planking supported by the bullet-torn uprights, the timber began to sag. Then with a rending of snapped wood, it gave way . . . and the armoured car hurtled to the track below.

" Greg !" It was Bell who gave the sudden warning. " A diesel train—coming along the track !"

" Quick, climb down the supports," Greg rapped. " It may be heading in the direction of the frontier—one of the inter-Continental expresses. If we can stop it. . . ."

He did not finish. All three were skimming down the wooden framework, racing to reach the track. Greg dropped alongside the rails. In the distance he sighted the diesel engine and behind it a stream of coaches.

How could they board it? A rapid glance round, and he yelled to Steve and Bell, " Lay those smashed timbers from the bridge across the rails. The driver will spot the obstruction in plenty of time to pull up."

The wrecked armoured car was piled in a smashed heap at one side of the track. Rushing to the timbers, they laid them just where it would appear that the crashed vehicle had caused them to block the line.

"Okay," Greg gasped. "Back along the track and get out of sight in the bushes. Hurry, chaps, hurry!"

They dived to cover as the diesel rounded a long curve. The scream of hastily applied brakes rent the air and the powerful locomotive slowed to a shuddering halt yards from the piled timber on the rails.

"Look, the crew is getting down, running to the armoured car," Greg snapped. "And the men from the train's mail van are leaping down to join 'em."

He parted the bushes. The mail van, its double-doors pushed apart by the postal officials who were now racing to the wrecked vehicle, was almost opposite the spot where the three crouched.

Greg nodded. It was a signal to the others to dart after him out of the bushes and through the open doors of the mail van. A quick glance along the track to make sure that the men from the train had their backs to them, and all three leapt into the van.

" Under that pile of empty mail bags," Greg snapped.

They crawled under the bags heaped in a corner. Minutes ticked past, then came the sounds of the postal crew returning and the doors were slid shut. The train moved forward.

Greg figured it would take two or three hours for the diesel-powered train to reach the frontier. Suddenly a tense feeling of anxiety gripped him as he lay hidden under the empty mail sacks. The train was slowing down. All three heard the van doors sliding apart.

Cautiously Greg peered out. He gave a start of dismay!

Through the open doors he saw a crowded platform. Drawn up beside them was a mail trolley. His eyes fastened on the name of the station on a large board, in front of which stood a group of armed soldiers.

The name on the board read LONZ!

They were back in Lonz! Instead of heading for the frontier the train had been going in the opposite direction; and on the platform were ZARB's soldiers.

"Steve, Bell," he hissed just loud enough for his voice to carry to the hidden men. "We're in Lonz. ZARB's guards are on the platform. They may search the train for us."

Hardly had he whispered the warning than the patrol moved towards the mail van. Greg knew they would search every inch of it—the empty sacks would be hurled aside and the three undercover agents were certain to be discovered!

The postal crew stepped back into the van, about to toss the mail bags on to the trolley on the platform. Two of them approached the empty sacks and started to drag them from the pile. In a few more moments Greg and the others would be exposed—and captured!

Greg's hand flashed to his wrist watch. He turned the tiny control operating its concealed transmitter. At once the watch's quiet tick became an amplified tick-tock, tick-tock, echoing loudly from under the pile of empty sacks.

A startled gasp reached him. He heard

one of the two men leap back in alarm. A scared yell filled the van.

"Run, there's a time-bomb hidden under these sacks."

Feet pounded to the door and thudded to the platform. Panic seized those outside and Greg could hear shouts and the noises of frightened men pounding away from the mail van.

"Quick," he hissed, heaving the sacks aside. "Come on."

He leapt across to the opposite side of the van and slid open the door. Steve and Bell darted after him as he leapt down to the track.

Crack! A bullet smashed into the track at Greg's feet. He flashed a hurried glance up at a footbridge. A ZARB guard had seen them and was sniping from the bridge. The sound of the shot caused the soldiers on the platform on the other side of the train, to snap into action.

"Dive under that other train," Greg yelled, jumping across a set of rails and hurling himself under a stationary train on another track.

All three threw themselves flat under one

of the coaches. They were out of range of the sniper on the footbridge. At that instant the train began to move. Within a few seconds it would have left the station. They would be exposed and a sitting target for both the sniper and the other enemy soldiers who were now racing towards them.

"Grab the rods," and as he shouted the words Greg was reaching up, his powerful hands gripping at the under-rods of the coach.

"Made it," Steve gasped, casting a grim eye on Bell. He breathed with relief as he saw him swinging on a set of rods and pulling himself clear of the track.

The train rumbled out of the station, running up a slight incline a few feet above a road which travelled parallel with the tracks.

"Greg! Look!"

Steve's sudden shout of alarm made Greg twist round to gaze back along the road at the side of the track.

Whizzing after the train was an open car containing a driver and two peak-capped soldiers. One of them was standing up gripping the side of the car while his eyes roved along the train. Greg saw his mouth open in a yell to his companions. He had caught sight of them clinging to the rods under the train.

The car accelerated and came level with the coach under which they were hanging.

"They're going to attack," Bell shouted.

The two soldiers were now leaning over the side of the car while the driver kept it parallel with the coach. The underside of the coach was at eye level with the car on the road.

The soldiers were armed with revolvers. Their shots were wild, the snipers thrown off-balance by the swaying of the car; but Greg knew that with the killers so close they must, sooner or later, find their targets.

Wrapping his legs tightly round the rod to which he was clinging, Greg snatched a thin metal tube from its holster in his trouser leg. He slipped a tiny glass capsule into the tube, put it to his mouth and waited.

The car steered nearer to the track. The two gunmen raised their revolvers, gripping their shooting arms with their free hands to steady their aim. Greg knew their shots would almost certainly thud home, smashing into the suspended body of one or more of the three.

He took a deep breath, sucking the glass capsule back to the tip of his lips. With an immense blow, he sent it down the thin tube.

With deadly flight the capsule spun from under the coach straight on to the bonnet of the speeding car. The force of its impact burst it. A split second's pause—and thick, choking, black smoke poured from the exploded capsule.

The three watched in triumph as the car swerved. The driver could see nothing and Greg knew that he and the two killers behind him were gasping for air. The car bounded off the road, hit a ditch and rolled over.

The train roared on. From Bell came a sudden gasp, and a strangled groan.

" Sorry—can't hold on—much longer."

Greg twisted his head in alarm. Bell had suffered a lot from the blow on his head. It was again telling on him. Somehow, he must stop the train before Bell's grip slackened.

Steve saw Greg edge to the side of the coach, reach up to the running board, and

The car bounded off the road ...

daringly pull himself up. He disappeared from Steve's anxious gaze.

Greg lay on the running board, put up his hand and grasped the handle of a door. He hauled himself upright. The coach window was open and startled faces peered out at him. He ignored them. His hand darted to the communication cord and gave it a terrific pull.

Instantly, the emergency brakes went into action and the train shuddered to a stop. Greg dropped to the track to find Steve and Bell already crawling from under the coach.

"Into the bushes at the side of the track," Greg gasped breathlessly, leading the way. "We've got to get clear of the track before they can start a hunt for us. There may be enemy soldiers on the train."

They sped at right angles to the track, beat a path through thick scrub, dashed into a wood, pounding between its close-growing trees until, at last, Bell was so breathless that they were forced to halt.

"Phew," Bell panted, holding his ribs and sucking in mighty gulps of air. "If you hadn't stopped—the train, Greg—guess I would have tumbled—under the wheels."

" You all right, now?" Greg asked anxiously and Bell nodded. " Then listen, Bell. You were about to tell us ZARB's secret plan when that mortar bomb exploded on the roof of your hut and k.o.'d you. What is ZARB's scheme?"

Bell took a long breath, eyeing them both grimly.

" ZARB called his agents to his headquarters to give each of them a small package. By now, those agents will be returning to their secret posts. Each agent has been ordered to drop his package into the sewers of the town to which he has been sent."

Greg gave a start, recalling ZARB's huge wall map of the world with its flags.

" What is in the packages?" Greg rapped.

Bell's reply brought gasps of dismay from both Steve and Greg.

" Micro-hydrogen bombs! BUT—they can be triggered off only by ZARB himself! At zero hour plus two, he will pull a switch in his castle headquarters. That switch will transmit a secret high-frequency radio control beam. The hydrogen bombs can only be detonated by that secret radio beam."

" But—what about his secret agents?"

" Zero hour is the time they have to drop the packages into the sewers. They each then have two hours to leave the town in high-powered cars. They must get clear away before zero plus two."

Greg took a deep breath to control his cold anger at ZARB's terrible scheme. He snapped another question at Bell.

" WHY is ZARB doing this? What is behind his horrible plan?"

" The micro-hydrogen bombs are to be exploded in small towns in the most wealthy countries of the world. They are to be warning of what ZARB can do—IF those countries do not pay ZARB huge sums in gold."

" But," Steve protested, " instead of paying the murdering villain they could launch attacks against him! They could wipe him out with bombers!"

" No," Bell shook his head. " That is where ZARB is extra cunning. None of the countries will know the identity of the secret saboteur, nor which country is responsible for exploding the micro-hydrogen bombs."

"Then," Greg demanded, "how is he going to collect the gold bullion ransoms?"

"He will order each country to deliver its ransom of gold by ship to a submarine at a rendezvous point in the Timan Sea. If they refuse, or try to destroy or track the submarine, far more terrible hydrogen bombs will be triggered off in the country which dares to defy ZARB."

Greg and Steve eyed Bell grimly. Greg snapped a question.

"Why does ZARB want all this gold?"

"ZARB plans to create the biggest army and air force in the Central continent! He wants gold to buy weapons and planes to equip the most modern army in the world. ZARB's evil ambition is to be a great dictator."

Greg's fists clenched, his eyes glinting with icy determination. "ZARB must be destroyed," he gritted. "With ZARB wiped out, his agents would be helpless. BUT— we haven't any time to lose. ZARB has to be eliminated *at once*!"

The others stared at him, wondering

how it was possible to carry out Greg's threat. He seemed to be unaware of their intent gazes.

His head was on one side, his ear cocked. He had heard a faint, distant throbbing. Greg's jaw tightened.

"Can you hear it?" he rapped, and they shook their heads, puzzled. "Helicopter. Must be the same machine that tried to knock us out on the viaduct. Hunting us again!"

Now Steve and Bell could hear it—it was circling steadily nearer.

"Listen," Greg ordered in a cool voice. "ZARB is desperate to get my camera because he knows it contains a photograph of his wall map and its tell-tale flags. He must have commanded the chopper pilot to find us and get the camera."

By now the helicopter's distant throb had become a loud roar. It was carrying out a wide, searching sweep over the countryside in a desperate attempt to locate the three daring British agents. Greg's lips twisted in a brief but grim smile.

"We're going to help that chopper pilot to find us," he snapped, and they gaped.

"Look, there's an open stretch of country just beyond those trees." The others nodded. "I'm going to run across it, as though dashing to the trees on the far side. The chopper crew will spot me."

"But they'll open fire on you," Steve gasped.

"Yes," and Greg's expression was cool and steady. "The instant they open fire, I'm going to drop as though shot. The pilot will land his chopper. One of his crew will run to the spot where I'm lying 'dead' to search my body for the camera."

"Just as he reaches me, Steve, set off this fire-cracker," and he handed a small cylinder to Steve.

With that, Greg raced out of the trees. The helicopter was circling overhead. The pilot immediately saw the figure running across the open country—a burst of rapid fire roared from the machine and the ground around Greg was spattered with bullets.

Greg threw up his arms and fell on his back. Steve and Bell tensed. Had Greg been hit? Or was he foxing?

The helicopter hovered above Greg, then with a swoop it landed a short distance from the still body. Steve and Bell saw a member of its crew, carrying a revolver, leap to the ground and run to the spot where Greg lay still.

Steve gave a start. In his anxiety he had all but forgotten Greg's command to set off the fire-cracker.

Hastily he hurled it into the trees behind him. A crackle of what sounded like shots drummed through the wood.

The man with the revolver had reached Greg and was about to stoop over him when the rapid firing broke out. He jerked round while the helicopter pilot and his navigator swung in their seats to stare over their shoulders.

In a flash, Greg was on his feet, his bunched fist crashing into the searcher's jaw. The man dropped, stunned. Greg snatched his revolver and leapt to the helicopter. As the startled crew swung back they found themselves staring into the muzzle of the revolver in Greg's hand.

" Out!" he roared at them, his voice savage and threatening. As they climbed out, eyeing him fearfully, Steve and Bell sped from the trees. " Bell, you're an experienced pilot," Greg snapped, and when Bell nodded, he continued. "You take the controls."

In seconds they were airborne, leaving the crew staring up at them in helpless fury. At Greg's command Bell lifted the machine high. Gazing over the countryside, Greg suddenly pointed. Bell nodded, and swung the helicopter in that direction.

A castle loomed on a distant hilltop. It was ZARB's headquarters.

"ZARB won't take any notice as we approach," Greg yelled to make himself heard above the roar of the rotor. "Take the chopper over the battlements and hover there for a few seconds. ZARB will think the crew is still searching for those three miserable British spies," he grinned.

As the helicopter approached the battlements Bell slackened speed and the machine hovered. Greg dropped the cable, leaving Steve at the winch control. He then issued a rapid order to Bell.

"I'm going down—keep circling. Steve, stand by the winch to haul me up."

With that, Greg slid down the cable and dropped lightly to the flat roof where earlier, he and Steve had outwitted ZARB's guards.

He waved to Bell who waved back then swooped the helicopter to circle above the castle.

Greg sped down the stone steps to the corridor, then crept along to the half-open door of ZARB's huge control room.

ZARB was at his massive desk, his gaze fastened on an electric wall clock, his outstretched hand hovering in front of a switch. On the desk was a small, square package. Grouped behind ZARB were men in high-ranking officers' uniforms.

"Ten minutes to zero plus two," Greg heard ZARB growl in a harsh, throaty voice, while with his free hand he picked up the square package. "Then, my officers, ZARB will lead you to the greatness of mighty military power."

Greg saw one of the officers eyeing the package nervously.

"Are you sure that micro-hydrogen bomb is not set?" he asked ZARB anxiously.

"Not for the radio beam which will trigger off the micro-bombs hidden by my secret agents in the foreign sewers," ZARB retorted. "Only a short wave beam could trigger this," he laughed savagely. Carelessly he tossed the package in his hand, while the men behind watched him with fear in their faces.

"He's mad," Greg gritted under his breath, as his gaze flitted round the large room. He looked at the clock.

Eight minutes to zero plus two! Against the wall behind ZARB and his officers was a radio control panel. Greg eyed it, measured the distance to it from the wall, and made a lightning decision. He switched on his micro-transmitter watch and whispered into it.

"Steve, tell Bell to hover in front of ZARB's control room. I want ZARB to spot the chopper's lowered cable!"

Tensely he waited until he heard the roar of the helicopter above the battlements. ZARB's head swung sharply to the large window. The men behind him turned to stare in the same direction.

Greg, crouching behind the open door, was watching them. As the cable swung into view, ZARB snarled furiously.

"What is that fool pilot doing?" he roared.

All eyes were on the window and the

cable beyond it. Greg slid through the doorway, sped on his toes along the wall and darted behind the radio control panel. He cast an anxious glance at the clock. Seven minutes to zero plus two.

Expertly and coolly he set to work. Twirling terminals, changing leads, he swiftly rerouted the control panel's wiring. A quick look at the clock told him it was six minutes to zero plus two.

ZARB swung his gaze back to his control switch. Out of the corner of his eye he saw that his door was now wide open. Greg saw him press another switch. With a muffled clang the door shut tight.

Greg's teeth clenched. He was trapped in the room. Only ZARB could open the door; and he and his men were all armed. Before Greg could reach it to try to force it open, he would be shot down, drilled through and through by bullets.

His eyes flashed to the window. It was shut. But outside hung the cable. Bell was still hovering above.

Greg gathered himself. With a rush, he streaked across the room, burst through the men standing between him and the closed

His flying body hurtled outwards . . .

window, folded his arms over his face, and leapt in a long, lightning dive.

C-rash! He smashed through the glass, shattering it as his flying body hurtled outwards. His arms shot forward, eyes wide open, and with a frantic snatch his powerful hands closed round the cable!

Steve, at the winch, gasped as he saw Greg flying in a shower of glass. Feverishly he swung in the cable, hauling Greg aboard.

"Bell, get this chopper moving," Greg roared. "Full throttle away from ZARB's castle," and he flashed a tense glance at his watch. Three minutes to zero plus two!

Bell opened the control to full power. The machine soared and hurtled up and away, clear of the castle, roaring at top speed, heading for the distant frontier.

Greg again looked at his watch.

Zero plus two!

A shattering boom thundered from the direction of the castle, now far in their rear. All three jerked round in their seats. A towering column of smoke and debris was soaring high into the air. Greg let out a huge breath.

"That's the end of ZARB," he shouted,

and as Bell and Steve stared at him with eager questions in their excited faces, he briefly explained.

"ZARB had one of his micro-hydrogen package bombs on his desk. I switched the controls of his radio panel. So, when ZARB pulled his desk switch, instead of triggering off the bombs which all his agents had planted, the radio control panel triggered the one on his own desk."

Steve stared at Greg with admiration.

"So ZARB destroyed himself," he cried. Greg nodded.

"That's what happened," he agreed. "And now we'll flip across the frontier, get my camera film printed and have those agents picked up."

And with a final glance back at the smoke cloud which marked the end of ZARB, the three daring British undercover agents roared on and across the frontier.